Piccolo Adventure Library
The Lost World

Piccolo Adventure Library

The Lost World

retold by Carey Miller from the original by Sir Arthur Conan Doyle
text and cover illustrations by Tom Barling
Piccolo Original Pan Books

First published 1977 by Pan Books Ltd,
Cavaye Place, London SW10 9PG
2nd printing 1978
Text © Pan Books Ltd 1977
Illustrations © Tom Barling 1977
ISBN 0 330 25133 3
Printed and bound in Great Britain by
Richard Clay (The Chaucer Press) Ltd, Bungay, Suffolk

1 Meeting the professor

It was a wet, foggy morning in the late spring when the three of us, clad in dripping mackintoshes, made our way up the gangplank of the great liner *Francisca* bound for South America. As our porter trundled ahead with a trolley piled high with trunks and guncases, I took the opportunity to cast a wary eye over my travelling companions. The younger man, Lord John Roxton, was stepping out briskly with his thin, eager face beaming through the gap between his hunting cap and muffler. But Professor Summerlee, a long melancholy man in his sixties, walked with dragging steps and drooping head, like one who was already feeling very sorry for himself! I knew exactly how he felt. I was also having doubts about embarking on the dangerous trip we had ahead of us. However, as this must be one of the most remarkable expeditions of all time, and as I may never return to England to explain how it all came about, I have decided to write an account of its beginning which will be sent back to my boss, the news editor of the *Daily Gazette*.

As Ned Malone, a junior reporter on the *Daily Gazette*, I had been sent by my news editor, Mr McArdle, to obtain an interview with a certain Professor George Challenger, a famous zoologist. The professor, apart from

claiming to have discovered some fierce and previously unknown animals in South America, was said to be quite mad and extremely violent. He was particularly well-known for his attacks on journalists, and only recently had fractured the skull of a *Telegraph* reporter while heaving him down the stairs. Certainly my own first meeting with the dangerous Professor Challenger is something I am unlikely to forget!

I had somehow managed to wangle this interview by writing a humble and respectful letter expressing great interest in the professor's theories (none of which I knew the first thing about). I did not, of course, admit to being a reporter. Much to my surprise he agreed to see me, and when I turned up on his doorstep at the appointed time I felt almost optimistic about the outcome of the meeting. I was in for a bigger surprise than I bargained for! I was shown into the professor's study where he was sitting in a rotating chair behind a broad table covered with books, maps and diagrams. As I entered, his chair spun round to face me. His appearance made me gasp. I was prepared for something strange, but nothing as over-powering as this. It was his size that took my breath away! His head was enormous, the largest I have ever seen on a human being. I am sure that his top hat, had I ever dared to try it on, would have slipped over my head entirely and rested on my shoulders. He had a face and beard that reminded me of a bull. His hair was peculiar, plastered down in front in a long, curving wisp over his massive forehead. His blue-black beard rippled down over his chest in the shape of a large spade. A huge expanse of shoulders and a chest like a barrel were the other parts

of him which appeared above the table, along with two enormous hands covered with long, black hair. Clear, critical eyes and a bellowing, rumbling voice completed my first impression of the notorious Professor Challenger.

'Well?' said he, with an insolent stare. I made a brief but valiant attempt to play my part as the interested young zoological student. But a few searching questions delivered by the professor in a calm but menacing voice soon revealed that I was a fraud and not a very clever one at that!

Once he had discovered this, the professor sprang to his feet with a mad rage in his eyes.

'Just as I suspected, another vile, crawling journalist! You have played a dangerous game here, Malone,' he shouted. 'And it strikes me that you have lost it!'

'Look here, sir,' I said, backing towards the door and opening it. 'I must ask you to keep your hands off me. I won't stand for it.'

'Dear me!' His black moustache lifted and a white fang twinkled in a sneer. 'You won't stand for it, eh?'

'Don't be a fool, professor!' I cried. 'I'm fifteen stone, as hard as nails, and play centre three-quarters for the London Irish. I'm not the man —'

At that moment he rushed me. It was lucky that I had opened the door or we should have gone right through it. We did a Catherine wheel together down the corridor, gathering up a chair on the way and bounding with it towards the street. My mouth was full of his beard, our arms were locked and the chair and our bodies were firmly entwined. The manservant, who seemed used to these events, flung open the front door, and we did a spectacular back somersault down the front steps and into the street. The chair splintered to matchwood as we hit

the ground and we finally came apart again in the gutter. The professor was the first to spring to his feet, wheezing and coughing but still waving his fists.

'Had enough?' he panted.

'You disgraceful bully!' I cried, as I pulled myself together, and the fight would have started all over again had it not been for the person now standing beside us. A policeman with a notebook.

'What's all this? You ought to be ashamed!' said the policeman, which seemed a reasonable thing to say under the circumstances.

'This man attacked me,' I said.

'Did you attack him?' the policeman asked the professor. Challenger breathed hard and said nothing.

'It's not the first time, either,' said the policeman sternly. 'You were in trouble last month for the same thing. You've given this young man a black eye. Do you want me to arrest him, sir?'

I suddenly changed my mind. 'No', I said, 'I do not!'

'What's that?' said the policeman.

'It was my fault. I gained entry into his house under false pretences. He did warn me!'

The policeman snapped shut his notebook.

'Let's have no more of it then,' he said, and began to move on the group of sightseers who had collected. The professor looked at me, and there was a twinkle in his eye that hadn't been there before.

'Come back inside,' he said. 'I haven't finished with you yet.' His words sounded sinister, but I followed him just the same. His wooden-faced manservant closed the door behind us.

2 An exciting discovery

We made our way along the corridor and re-entered the
room we had left so noisily ten minutes before. The
professor closed the door, pushed me towards an
armchair and offered me a cigar.

'I have invited you back into my house,' he announced,
'because you actually admitted to that policeman that you
were to blame. That shows a kind of honesty that I have
not come across before in members of the newspaper
profession. I have therefore decided that I will talk to you
about South America. Obviously it was to hear about that
that you came here in the first place. However, you must
give me your word of honour that nothing of what I tell
you will be published in any newspaper.' I was reluctant
to agree to this. Reporting the facts was my job, and I
knew there would be a great many people very interested
to hear the true story behind the professor's discoveries.
But it was pretty obvious that he would turn me out
again if I didn't agree and so, since by now I was very
curious, I finally promised to keep silent.

'In the first place,' began the professor 'you are probably
aware that I made a trip to South America two years ago.
You may also be aware that the country round some parts
of the Amazon is still only partly explored. I needed to
visit this little-known back-country to study the animals

of the region for a book I am writing on the subject. On
the way back after finishing my work, I called in at a small
Indian village where I was asked to give medical aid to a
very sick man. Unfortunately the man died the instant
I entered his hut. But the surprising thing was that he
was not an Indian but a blond-haired, pale-skinned
white man. He was dressed in rags, painfully thin and
had obviously suffered great hardship. The Indians said

he was a complete stranger to them and had staggered into their village and collapsed unconscious. I examined the poor man's knapsack which was lying beside him and found that it was labelled "Maple White, Lake Avenue, Detroit, Michigan". The dead man seemed to have been an artist and poet for there were scraps of poetry and crayons in the knapsack and a sketchbook in his shirt pocket!'

Professor Challenger produced this sketchbook and handed it to me. I leafed through several colourful landscapes before coming to a full-page picture of the most extraordinary creature I had ever seen in my life. It was like a nightmare! The head resembled that of a fowl with the body of a bloated lizard and a long, spiky tail. The curved back was edged with a high, saw-toothed fringe which looked like a dozen cock's combs placed one behind the other. In front of this monster was a tiny dwarf-like figure, who stood staring up at it.

When I questioned the professor about the strange picture he claimed that the grotesque animal was a type of dinosaur called a stegosaurus, and had obviously been drawn from life by the dead man. I would have burst out laughing had it not been for the thought that I might get thrown downstairs again! However, the professor could see that I didn't believe him and he began to produce various pieces of evidence to support his astonishing claim. The first of these was a six-inch-long bone with dried cartilage at the end of it which, he claimed, could only have come from the foot of a very large and probably fierce creature like the one in the drawing. He also produced a blurred and damaged photograph of what appeared to be a large bird sitting on a tree. Professor

Challenger then told me that he had actually shot and
killed the thing in the tree and had attempted to bring it
home with him. But during the return journey his boat
had overturned, ruining many other photos, and the body
of the dead creature had been swept over the rapids and
lost. However, when the half-drowned professor later

scrambled ashore, he found he had a piece of the strange creature's wing still clutched in his hand. Then from a drawer in his desk he produced what seemed to be the upper part of the wing of a large bat. It was at least two feet in length and had a curved bone with a piece of thick, transparent tissue underneath it.

'A monstrous bat?' I suggested.

'Nothing of the sort,' said the professor severely. He opened a large, illustrated book and handed it to me.

'Here,' he said, pointing to the picture of an extra-ordinary flying monster. 'This is an excellent drawing of the pterodactyl, a flying reptile of the Jurassic period. On the next page is a diagram of a wing. Please compare it with the wing you have in your hand.' As I did so a wave of utter amazement passed over me. I was really convinced; the proof was overwhelming! I realized that the poor professor had been totally misjudged, and I told him so.

'It's the most exciting discovery I have ever known,' I said. 'When everyone hears the truth you will be hailed as the Christopher Columbus of science who has really discovered a lost world! But if what you say is true, how could these prehistoric animals have survived for so long? And how is it that no one has discovered them before?'

'There can only be one explanation,' said the professor. 'South America is a granite continent: in the past there must have been a sudden volcanic eruption and an area as large as the county of Sussex seems to have been pushed up in one large lump with all its living contents still on top. This plateau is so high above the rest of the land, and the cliffs on which it is perched are so steep, that it has been completely cut off from civilization. So

creatures and vegetation have survived on it that would otherwise have disappeared long ago. The pterodactyl and the stegosaurus are from the Jurassic period and therefore date from a very distant time in the history of the world. They have been artificially preserved by a strange and unlikely accident. I tried to find a way up to the top of this precipice, and did in fact manage to get half way. That is where I shot the flying reptile. I am convinced that somewhere there must be a way up to the plateau. Maple White obviously knew it; he must have reached the summit to make his drawing of the stegosaurus. If only he had lived long enough to tell the tale!'

'The thing I don't understand,' I said, 'is why you haven't presented this evidence to the authorities?'

'I have tried,' said the professor bitterly. 'But I am not a patient man. When I was met with disbelief and stupidity I began to get extremely angry and violent, as you have discovered this morning.' I rubbed my throbbing eye and said nothing.

'Tonight, however, I am attending a lecture in the Zoological Institute Hall where I am to give a vote of thanks to the speaker. I shall take the opportunity then of saying something about my discoveries, and I am hoping to convince some people at least that I am telling the truth.'

'And may I come along?' I asked eagerly.

'Why, surely,' he answered warmly. His happy smile was a wonderful thing, his cheeks became two red apples between his half-closed eyes and the great black beard.

'By all means come. It will be a comfort to me to know that I have one ally in the hall. Remember though, that you must say nothing to your editor about this

20

interview. You can inform him that if he sends any more reporters here I shall call on him with a riding whip. Good morning!'

3 A rash decision

Back at the offices of the *Gazette*, it was difficult to explain away my bruises to Mr McArdle, the news editor. It was even harder to convince him that Challenger was not the fraud that everyone thought he was. When I told him that none of my amazing interview was for publication, he was quite incredulous. He obviously thought that the knock on the head had affected my brain. However, he grudgingly agreed that I might attend the zoological meeting. Obviously he hoped that something sensational might happen that we could print.

I told Tarp Henry, my close friend and fellow journalist, about my meeting with the violent professor and asked him to come to the lecture with me. He quickly dismissed Challenger's story as rubbish and said he had probably got the pterodactyl bone out of an Irish stew! But he thought there might be a bit of a commotion at the Queen's Hall, so he said he would come along to see the fun. We were both surprised to find so many other people with the same idea. The hall was crowded with men and women from all walks of life, both old and young, plus a large number of medical students. The mood seemed to be one of suppressed excitement. Were all these people here to listen to a rather dull lecture? Or was the enthusiastic turnout due to the fact that the notorious mad professor was taking part?

Mr Waldron, the speaker, gave us a talk on what seemed to be a bird's eye view of creation – as seen by the scientists. All went well while he talked, at some length, about the lowest molluscs and simplest sea-creatures. From there he went on to reptiles, fishes and then the kangaroo-rat. It was when he got on to 'those large horrific lizards that were, fortunately, extinct before the appearance of man' that the trouble really started. Professor Challenger began to heckle poor Mr Waldron in that booming, bellowing voice of his that was so hard to ignore. The hall was soon in an uproar. Many people roared with laughter whilst others howled 'Shame!', 'Put him out!' and 'Shove him off the platform!' Poor Mr Waldron, although a very experienced lecturer and certainly no coward, became more and more rattled. He stumbled, repeated himself and finally brought his lecture to an untimely end.

Professor Challenger then stood up amid boos and cheers. Instead of thanking Mr Waldron for the lecture, as he was meant to, he told him that many of his so-called 'facts' were inaccurate. He also said that Mr Waldron was very wrong in supposing that just because he hadn't seen any, prehistoric animals no longer existed.

'I know such monsters exist because I have seen some of them,' he boomed, 'and they are large and fierce enough to devour any of the puny animals that Mr Waldron knows of.' Howls of 'Rubbish!' and 'Prove it!' came from the audience. The professor attempted to carry on calmly, but his face was flushed and his beard bristling. It

24

was obvious to me that he would go berserk at any moment. The whole audience seethed and simmered like a boiling pot, and several nervous ladies made a hasty exit. The professor took a step forward and raised both his hands. There was something so big and powerful about this strange figure that the shouting died away at once.

'I will not keep you,' he said. 'It is not worth it. I know I am speaking the truth but you don't believe me.' The audience cheered.

'Then I shall put you to the test,' he said, 'Let me have two volunteers to go and test my statements in South America!' There was a sudden hush and all heads turned to see if anyone would be foolish enough to offer himself. Mr Summerlee, the Professor of Comparative Anatomy, a withered and bitter looking man, came slowly forward to the accompaniment of more cheers from the audience. Professor Challenger was delighted, and assured the older man that he would give him detailed directions for finding his way to the world of the dinosaurs.

'But you must remember,' Challenger rumbled on, 'that there will be many difficulties and dangers facing Mr Summerlee. He will need a younger and stronger man to go with him. Can I ask for a volunteer?'

I suddenly found that I was on my feet and speaking although no words seemed to be coming out. My friend, Tarp Henry, was pulling me down by the coat tails and I heard him whispering:

'Sit down, Malone! Don't make a complete fool of yourself!' At the same time I was aware that a tall, gaunt man with gingery hair, a few seats in front of me, was also on his feet. He glared back at me with angry eyes like

blue ice chips. But I refused to give way.

'I will go, Mr Chairman,' I kept repeating over and over again.

'Name! Name!' cried the audience.

'My name is Edward Dunn Malone. I am a reporter on the *Daily Gazette*. I claim to be an absolutely unprejudiced witness.'

'What is your name, sir?' the chairman asked my tall rival.

'I am Lord John Roxton,' his voice rang out confidently. 'I have already been up the Amazon. I know the ground and have special qualifications for this investigation!'

'If you are Lord John Roxton then your reputation as a sportsman and a traveller is, of course, known to the whole world,' said the chairman. 'At the same time it

would be useful to have a member of the press like Mr
Malone on such an expedition.'

'Then I move,' said Professor Challenger, 'that *both*
these gentlemen should be elected to go with Professor
Summerlee on his expedition to prove that what I say is
true.'

And so, amid wild shouting and cheering, my fate was
sealed. I was so stunned by the situation into which I had
recklessly thrown myself, that I hardly felt my body being
swept away in the human current that swirled towards the
door. I reeled along Regent Street thinking about my
future, if indeed I had any, when a hand touched my arm.
I turned, and found myself looking into the eyes of the
tall, lean man who had volunteered to go with me on this
unlikely quest.

'Mr Malone, I understand,' said he. 'We are to be companions then. I live just near here. Could you spare me a half hour of your time? I really would like to get to know you better.'

4 Doorway to the unknown

Our voyage on the *Francisca* was luxurious and relaxing, and it gave the three of us time to get to know each other. I had already taken a strong liking to Lord John, having spent the rest of that fateful evening at his flat. I had enjoyed his company enormously. Years before I met him I had read a lot about him, for he was world-famous for his exploits in Brazil and Peru. On one trip, several years before, he had become involved in a fight between a handful of villains and the Indians they were treating as slaves. These rogues had practised the most inhuman tortures on the poor natives in order to force them to gather india rubber. It ended with Lord John killing the leader of the villains, Pedro Lopez, with his own hands. Since then Lord Roxton had been acclaimed as a hero in some parts of South America. He was an odd-looking man in his thirties with strange, twinkling, restless eyes of a pale, frosty blue. His nose was strongly curved and his face looked haggard in spite of its deep tan. He must have been at least six feet tall but his hunched, rounded shoulders made him seem much shorter. I felt he was a man I could trust with my life, just the man to have on your side in a tight corner.

Professor Summerlee was not quite so easy to get along with. I found him acid tempered and fault finding, and he made no secret of his belief that Professor Challenger was an absolute fraud. He was convinced that we had embarked on a crazy wild goose chase that could bring nothing but disappointment and danger. This opinion, which he repeated endlessly and passionately with much wagging of his thin, goat-like beard, did nothing to cheer up my flagging spirits! However, Professor Summerlee turned out to be better suited than I had thought to this sort of gruelling expedition. Although in his 66th year, his gaunt, stringy body was wiry and strong and he never showed the slightest sign of tiredness. I felt sure that when the going got rough his powers of endurance would be quite equal to mine!

On the gloomy dawn of the day we left for South America, Professor Challenger came down to the dock to see us off. He gave us a sealed envelope which contained all the directions we would need for our quest. We were to open the envelope when we reached a town on the banks of the Amazon called Manaos. On no account must the envelope be opened before the exact date and time written on the outside. Although this seemed an odd request, Professor Summerlee finally agreed to it.

After leaving the liner we spent a week at a place called Para, getting our equipment ready. Here we engaged Gomez and Manuel, two Spanish Indians from up-river. They were tough-looking fellows, bearded, fierce and as supple and wiry as panthers. Both of them had spent their lives in the part of the Amazon that we wanted to explore, so they seemed very suitable for the job in hand. One of them, Gomez, could also speak perfect English. Besides these we engaged three Bolivians who were used to working on the river and one powerfully built black African called Zambo.

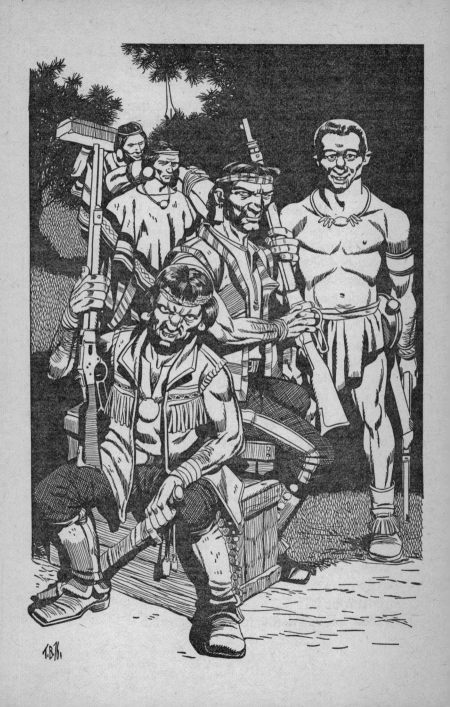

From Para we all travelled by steamer up a slow-moving river the colour of clay, until we reached the town of Manaos. When we arrived we were invited to spend a few nights at the house of a representative of the British and Brazilian Trading Company. At last, after a weary week, the day and the hour arrived for us to open the envelope that would start us on our dangerous trek into unknown country.

We sat in the shaded sitting room of the villa Santa Ignacio. Outside we were surrounded by the brassy glare of the sun and the black shadows of the palm trees. The air was filled with the hum of insects, ranging from the deep drone of the bee to the high piping note of the mosquito. We pulled our chairs around a cane table in the middle of the room. On it lay the sealed envelope bearing the words:

Instructions to
Lord John Roxton and party.
To be opened at Manaos upon July 15th
at 12 o'clock precisely.

Lord John had placed his watch on the table beside him. He looked at it and then took the envelope and slit it open with his pen-knife. From it he drew a folded piece of paper which he carefully opened and spread upon the table. It was blank. He turned it over. The other side too was blank. We looked at each other in a bewildered silence which was broken by a sneering laugh from Professor Summerlee.

'Well, the fellow has proved himself to be a fraud. Now we can return to England and show him up for the impostor he is!'

'Perhaps it's invisible ink?' I suggested.

'I'm afraid not,' said Lord John, holding the paper up to the light. 'I'll swear nothing has ever been written on this piece of paper.

'May I come in?' boomed a voice from the verandah. The shadow of a squat figure had stolen across the patch of sunlight. That voice! Those monstrous shoulders! We sprang to our feet with a gasp of astonishment as Challenger, wearing a round straw hat with a coloured ribbon, filled the open space before us.

'I'm afraid,' he said, taking out his watch, 'that I am a few minutes late. When I gave you the envelope, I fully intended to arrive before you opened it, but I got rather delayed on the river. My stupid pilot drove into a sandbank. Are you ready for your journey?'

'We can start tomorrow,' I said.

'Then so you shall. You need no chart now, for you have me to guide you. That will, of course, be a great advantage. From now on,' he declared, 'I intend to take full charge of this expedition. Since my time is valuable, I suggest we push on as rapidly as possible. I'm sorry I didn't travel with you but I really do prefer my own company, you know!'

Lord John had chartered a large steam launch, the *Esmerelda*, which was to carry us up the river. In this part of the world there is a wet season from December to May when the river becomes very swollen and treacherous. Fortunately the waters begin to go down again in June and we were able to navigate the river in normal conditions. In fact, thanks to the powerful engines of the *Esmerelda*, our trip up the Amazon was no more difficult than crossing a stagnant lake. For three days we steamed westward up a stream which was so enormous that from its centre the banks were mere shadows on the distant skyline. On the

33

fourth day we turned into a narrower tributary and two days later we arrived at a small Indian village. Professor Challenger insisted that we land here and send the steamer back to Manaos. We would soon be coming to rapids where a large boat would be useless.

The *Esmerelda* turned back on August 2nd and we bought two large, light canoes from the villagers to continue our journey. We also hired two of the local people, Ataca and Ipetu, to help us with the navigation. Apparently these were the two who had helped the professor on his previous trip.

I began to sense the mounting excitement among us. At that moment we were standing in the doorway to the unknown. The next day we would disappear through it.

5 Jungle drums

Our possessions, we found, fitted very neatly into two
canoes. We split into two parties of six with a professor
in each. (This was done to cut down the amount of
bickering that always went on between them). I was in
Challenger's party and found him in a very pleasant
mood. I was still wary of him, however, as his good moods
rarely lasted long. For two days we made our way up a
broad, dark-coloured river. Twice we came to rapids and
had to carry the canoes for half a mile or so overland. I
shall never forget those majestic and mysterious forests
that grew thick on both sides of the river. The trees were
thicker than anything I had seen in my town-bred life.
They shot upwards in magnificent columns until, at some
enormous distance above our heads, we could dimly see
where they joined to make one great matted roof.
Occasionally a tiny, golden ray of sunshine would shoot
down to earth, making a dazzling line of light in the deep
green. There were vivid flowers and wonderfully coloured
plants and lichens growing on the barks of the trees.
After the drab grey London streets, this place seemed like
fairyland.

We saw no animal life, yet a continuous movement at the
tops of the trees made us aware of the hundreds of pairs
of eyes watching in amazement as the dark figures

stumbled along so far below. At dawn and sunset the howler monkeys screamed and the parakeets chattered. But during the hot hours of the day only the perpetual drone of insects, like the beating of distant surf, filled our ears.

On the third day we heard a new sound, a kind of deep throbbing that came and went throughout the morning. The two boats were paddling along, a few yards apart, when we first heard it. Our Indians remained completely still, as if turned to bronze, watching intently with terror in their eyes.

'What is it?' I asked.

'War drums,' said Lord John casually. 'I have heard them before.'

'Yes sir, war drums,' said Gomez. 'Wild Indians, they watch us every mile of the way. Kill us if they can.'

'How can they watch us?' I asked, gazing out into dark nothingness. Gomez shrugged.

'The Indians know. They have their own way. They watch us. They talk drum talk to each other. Kill us if they can.'

By the afternoon of that day at least six or seven drums were throbbing from various points, some asking questions, others answering them. One to the east made a rattle like a machine gun, whilst one in the north rumbled like a threat of thunder. The longer it went on, the more spine-chilling it became. I could almost hear them beating out the words *We will kill you if we can. We will kill you if we can.* Yet in the silent woods there was no sign of movement. The Indians wandered around in a state of shock, but the professors carried on quarrelling, as loudly as usual, and all around us nature seemed at peace. Behind the curtain of vegetation the

drums rumbled and whispered all day.

We will kill you if we can. We will kill you if we can.

That night we moored our canoes in the centre of the stream and prepared for possible attack. But nothing came, and when the sun rose we pushed on, leaving the sound of the drums rumbling distantly behind us.

At about three in the afternoon, we came to a very steep rapid, more than a mile long. Professor Challenger told us this was the very place that he had overturned his canoe and lost the pterodactyl. I was relieved to hear this as it was the first bit of evidence, however tiny, that Challenger was telling the truth, and that we were really on the right trail. We made our way around the rapids,

and about ten miles further on we decided to anchor for
the night. Next day Challenger was excited to discover a
very important landmark, an Assai palm, jutting out from
the bank at a distinctive angle.

'The secret opening is half a mile onwards on the other
side of the river,' he told us. 'There is no break in the
trees. That is the mysterious thing about it. When you
can see light green rushes instead of dark green
undergrowth, that is my private gate into the unknown.
Push through it and its secret will be yours too!'

It was indeed a wonderful place, the most magical and
fascinating that man could imagine. As we poled our
canoes through the opening in the pale green rushes, the

thick leaves closed over us, making a green and golden tunnel over the transparent stream. Clear as crystal, motionless as glass, green as the edge of an iceberg, the water stretched in front of us. Every stroke of our paddles sent a thousand ripples across its shiny surface. There was no sign of the Indian drums here, and many more animals began to show themselves. They were so tame that it was obvious they had not seen enough of man to fear him. We saw fuzzy, black-velvet monkeys with snow-white teeth and gleaming eyes; we also saw crocodiles plunging heavily into the water. Once we saw a tapir staring at us through a gap in the rushes. Another time it was a great puma, whose green eyes glittered through the brush-wood. Bird life was plentiful, especially the wading birds, stork, heron and ibis, who stood in groups on every log that jutted out from the bank. The crystal water beneath us was alive with fish of every shape and colour.

For three days we made our way up this tunnel of hazy green sunshine. The deep peace of our magic waterway was unbroken by any sign of man.

'No Indian here. Too much afraid *Curupuri*,' said Gomez.

'*Curupuri* is the spirit of the woods,' explained Lord John. 'It's their name for any kind of devil or evil spirit.' In spite of the day's warmth, I shivered.

On the third day the boats began to scrape on the bottom of the river and Challenger told us that they would no longer be of use to us. From now on we would have to walk. We pulled them out of the water and hid them under some thick bushes, marking the nearest tree with an axe so that we would be able to find them again. Then we shared out the luggage between us – guns, ammunition, food, blankets and a tent. With our burdens on our backs we then embarked on the last and most difficult stage of the journey.

We walked like this for nine long days. At last we began to leave the trees behind, and entered a wilderness of bamboo. It grew so thickly that we had to cut a pathway for ourselves with broad-bladed Indian knives called machetes. It took us a long day from 7 in the morning till 8 at night, to get through this obstacle. It was tiring and monotonous. My vision throughout the day was limited to the back of Lord John's cotton jacket in front of me and the towering wall of bamboo at either side. I couldn't imagine what sort of creatures could live in that dense thicket, but several times we heard the sounds of large, heavy animals quite close to us.

Early next morning we were off again across a plain and down into a valley. After this we began to cross a series of hills, and it was while we were crossing the first of these that something rather curious happened. Professor Challenger stopped suddenly and pointed excitedly to the right. As he did so we saw, about a mile away, a huge grey bird flap slowly up from the ground and skim smoothly off, flying low and straight, until it was lost among the tree ferns.

'Did you see it?' cried Challenger triumphantly. 'Summerlee, did you see it?'

The other man was staring at the spot where the creature had disappeared. 'What do you claim it was?' he asked.

'Why, a pterodactyl, of course,' said Challenger.

Summerlee cackled with laughter. 'A ptero-fiddlestick!' said he. 'It was a stork if ever I saw one!'

Challenger was too furious to speak. He swung his pack on his back and marched on. I hadn't seen the bird at all, but Lord John, who had watched it through his binoculars, told me that it was quite unlike any bird he had ever seen before!

At last our destination lay in full view. When we had crossed the second ridge and set up camp, we saw before us an irregular plain studded with palm trees and then a long line of high, red cliffs. It was six or seven miles off and it curved away, stretching as far as I could see. Only one more day and all our doubts should be put to rest!

6 On the right track

That night we pitched our camp at the foot of the cliff – a wild and desolate spot. The crags above us were not only straight and sheer, they actually curved outwards at the very top. It made climbing them quite impossible. Close to us was a high, thin pinnacle of rock that looked like a red church spire. The top of it was level with the plateau but there was a gaping chasm in between them. On the summit of the peak grew a high tree.

'It was on that,' said Professor Challenger, pointing to this tree, 'that the pterodactyl was perched. I climbed half-way up the rock before I shot him.' As Challenger talked of his pterodactyl, I was surprised to see on the face of Professor Summerlee an expression which was not a sneer. For the first time he seemed to be listening to Challenger with real interest and excitement. Challenger saw it too, and began to grin as if he was just beginning to enjoy himself.

The following morning we held a council of war to decide the best method of climbing up to the plateau so far above us. Professor Challenger told us that on his previous expedition he had tried every possible method of scaling the rock face, without success. He had also surveyed the cliffs for six miles to the west without discovering even a foothold. He suggested that we should carry on moving

westward round the plateau in the hope that an entry might be found further along. After all, as Professor Challenger kept on pointing out, Maple White had got on and off the plateau. If he could do it, so could we!

No one had a better suggestion, so we broke camp and began walking to the west. The ground at the foot of the cliff was rocky and broken up, so the going was difficult and slow. Suddenly, however, we discovered something that cheered us up enormously. It was an old camp site with several empty meat tins, an old brandy bottle, a broken tin opener and other such rubbish. There was also a crumpled and rotting copy of a newspaper *The Chicago Democrat*! We had stumbled on Maple White's old camp!

Sure now that we were on the right track, we began to hurry. We came across a large patch of high bamboo which was growing at the foot of the cliff. Many of the stems were 20 feet tall, with sharp, strong points almost like spears. As we were passing, my eye was caught by the gleam of something white within it. I pushed my head between the stems and was horrified to find myself staring into the empty sockets of a fleshless skull!

The Indians cleared the bamboo away from the spot with their machetes and we found the rest of the skeleton lying a little further along. Only a few shreds of clothing remained on it, but there were still boots on the bony feet. They looked the type worn by Europeans. We also found a gold watch and chain and silver cigarette case, with 'J.C., from A.E.S.', on the lid. Challenger told us that Maple White had been travelling with another American called James Colver, who had not been heard of since White's death. Could these be the remains of James Colver?

'Well,' said Lord John, 'one thing is certain, and that is

how he met his death. He must have fallen from the top
of the cliff, or been thrown from it, and impaled himself
on the bamboo spikes. How else could he have broken
so many bones?'

A hush came over us as we stood around the shattered
skeleton and thought about the truth of Lord John's
words. Undoubtedly, the man had fallen from the
plateau. Or had he been thrown? Already horrific
possibilities were beginning to form in my mind. Odd
words kept coming into my head. '*Curupuri. We will kill
you if we can.*' I felt very uneasy.

We moved off in silence and continued our trek round
the line of the cliffs, which still seemed as even and
unbroken as a monstrous Arctic icefield. In 5 miles we
saw no rift or tiny break anywhere. Then, quite

unexpectedly, we saw a chalked white arrow. It had been drawn in a hollow of rock to protect it from the rain and it was pointing westward.

'Maple White again,' said Professor Challenger. 'I remember he had chalks in his kit-bag. Leaving a trail seems a very sensible idea.'

Five miles later we found another arrow. This time it was at a point where the face of the cliff had a narrow split in it. Inside this cleft was another arrow pointing upwards. Although we were by this time very hungry and tired we couldn't relax until we had investigated.

It was very dark inside the cleft, but we could just see a small circle that seemed darker than the rest. Lord John had a torch in his knapsack, and as he shone it into the hole we saw once again the sign of the chalk arrow, once more pointing upwards. Lord John climbed up first, shining his torch in front of him, and the rest of us filed behind. The tunnel appeared to have been worn by water, and had smooth sides and a floor covered with rounded stones. It was so narrow that to begin with we had to stoop, but we soon found we were crawling up it on our hands and knees!

Suddenly we heard a shout from Lord Roxton. 'It's blocked!' he cried. 'The roof has fallen in!'

Too depressed to speak we scrambled down again – out into daylight. The road that Maple White had taken was now closed, and with it had gone our only chance to see the mysterious land on top of the plateau. A dreadful blow!

As we stood in a miserable group at the mouth of the gorge, a huge boulder suddenly shot past us with tremendous force. It was a very narrow escape, for it could easily have killed us all. The Indians, who were standing out of sight, said that it had rushed past them too and appeared to have been thrown in our direction from the top. Very frightened, we left the area of the gorge as quickly as we could. Our mission now seemed quite impossible – yet with all that mystery only a few hundred feet above our heads, there wasn't one of us who could think of returning to London.

We decided to carry on trekking round the foot of the cliffs in the hope of finding another tunnel, until we reached our starting place. We walked for 22 miles the next day, but with no success at all. Our depression lifted a little that evening when Lord John managed to shoot an ajouti, a small pig-like animal which would make us a very tasty supper.

We were roasting this over the fire, huddling close to it to keep warm, when suddenly something swooped towards us with a noise like a light plane. For an instant the whole of our group was covered by a canopy of leathery wings. I caught a quick glimpse of a long snake-like neck, a fierce greedy eye and a great snapping beak, filled with tiny teeth that glittered. The next second it was gone – and so was our dinner! A huge black shadow, twenty feet across, blotted out the stars for a couple of seconds and then vanished over the brow of the high cliffs above us.

We sat around the fire in stunned silence. Summerlee was the first to speak.

'Professor Challenger,' he said, 'I owe you an apology, sir. I have been very wrong, and I do hope you will forgive my past mistakes.' For the first time the two professors shook hands and it was certainly worth a lost supper to get those two difficult men together!

For the next three days we travelled wearily on through

barren, forbidding country, part of it was stony desert, part desolate marsh. Many times we found ourselves up to our waists in the sludge and slime of an old, semi-tropical swamp.

These swamps seemed to be the breeding place of the Jaracaca snake, the fiercest reptile in South America. It attacks men on sight and its bite brings instant death. There were always far too many of them to shoot so we kept running until we were exhausted.

By the sixth day we were back at the first camp by the red pinnacle of rock, feeling very frustrated and gloomy. No one could have examined those cliffs more carefully than we had. We were certain that there was no place on that mighty rock that even a highly skilled acrobat could climb.

As we lay down to sleep that night, none of us could see any alternative to returning home empty-handed. The last thing I saw as I dropped off to sleep was Challenger squatting by the fire like a huge bullfrog. His heavy head was in his hands and he was sunk in deep thought.

But it was a different man that greeted us the next morning.

'Eureka!' he cried, his teeth shining through his beard. 'Gentleman – I have solved the problem!'

7 'This is no bird!'

After breakfast, and with the help of Professor
Challenger's climbing equipment, we began to climb the
pinnacle of rock that lay alongside the plateau. Challenger
and Lord John were experienced mountaineers and
Summerlee had done some rock-climbing, so I was the
only amateur. The climb was much easier than I had
expected, mainly because Challenger went up first and
let down a rope. He tied it to the very large tree that grew
on the pinnacle, and the rest of us heaved ourselves up
on it.

At the top was a grassy summit, quite flat and about
25 feet across. The first impression I had was of the
incredible view around us. The entire Brazilian plain
seemed to lie beneath us, stretching away and away until
it ended in a dim blue mist on the farthest skyline. Then
I turned to look at the plateau. It was exactly level with
the grass on which we stood, and it seemed so near that
I felt I could almost lean over and touch it.

'This is very curious,' said the creaking voice of Professor
Summerlee. I turned and found that he was examining
the large tree we had used in our ascent. The smooth bark
and those small ribbed leaves seemed very familiar.

'Why,' I cried, 'it's a beech!'

'Exactly,' said Summerlee. 'A friend in a far country.'

'Not just a friend, my good sir,' said Challenger. 'This beech tree will be our salvation.'

'By George!' cried Lord John. 'A bridge!'

It was certainly a brilliant idea. The tree was a good sixty feet high, and if only it could be made to fall the right way it would cross the chasm easily. Challenger handed me an axe, and under his instructions, I cut gashes in the sides of the tree that should make it fall in exactly the right place. Then I set to work in earnest upon the trunk, taking turns with Lord John.

In just over an hour there was a loud crack, and the tree swayed forward and crashed over, burying its branches in the bushes at the far side. The trunk rolled to the very

edge of our grassy platform, and for one terrible second we
thought it would go over. But it balanced itself, a few
inches from the edge, and we now had a bridge into the
unknown.

Before crossing, Lord John insisted that we should
bring up our ammunition and supply of rifles. After all, we
had already had plenty of signs of the trouble that might
be waiting for us. The Indians climbed up too, bringing a
large bale of provisions in case our exploration should be a
long one.

At last we were ready and Challenger shuffled across the
trunk and was soon at the other side. He clambered to
his feet and waved his arms in the air.

'At last,' he cried. 'At last!'

I gazed anxiously at him, feeling convinced that the *Curupuri* would dart out from behind the green curtain and devour him! Yet all was curiously quiet. Soon all four of us were actually there, standing in the lost world of Maple White. It seemed like a moment of triumph. But there was disaster to follow!

We had turned away from the edge and gone about 50 yards into the brushwood when there came an earsplitting crash behind us. We rushed back to the edge of the chasm. The bridge had gone! Far down at the base of the cliff, I saw a tangled mass of branches and a splintered trunk. It was our beech tree. Before we had time to realize the seriousness of this, we caught sight of a swarthy face peering across at us from the rocky pinnacle. It was Gomez, with flashing eyes and a sneer of hatred twisting his handsome features.

'Lord John Roxton!' he shouted. 'Lord John Roxton!'

'Well,' said my friend, 'here I am.'

A shriek of wild laughter echoed chillingly across the abyss.

'And there you will stay, you English dog. You found it hard to get up; you will find it harder to get down. You stupid fools, you are trapped, every one of you!' We were too astounded to speak.

'We nearly killed you with a stone at that cave,' Gomez cried. 'But this is better; it is slower and more terrible. Your bones will whiten up there and no one will know where to look for you. As you lie dying, think of Lopez, whom you shot 5 years ago on the Putomayo river. I am his brother, and come what will, I have avenged his memory and now I can die happy!'

He was to die sooner than he expected! Lord John

ran swiftly along the edge of the plateau and brought the man down with a single crack of his rifle. Then we saw the huge ebony figure of Zambo bounding downhill after the other Indian, Manuel. He picked him up like a doll and threw him over the edge of the pinnacle.

It was all over in a matter of seconds. Both traitors had been severely dealt with – but what was to become of us now? There was no possible way of returning to the pinnacle. We stood and waited in shocked silence for Zambo to return.

Soon his honest face and Herculean figure appeared again at the top of the crag.

'Whatever do I do now?' he asked. 'I do not wish to leave you!' Actually there was a lot he could do to help, and he was very willing. Using the rope, he managed to swing the packages of provisions and ammunition over to us. By the time he had finished, it was evening. He told us that the Indians were very unhappy about the Englishmen's predicament.

'Too much *Curupuri* live in this place,' they were saying. They had decided to return to their village. Zambo went back to the camp at the bottom of the pinnacle, while we rolled up in our blankets and fell into a shallow, uneasy sleep.

We saw Zambo again the following day when he came up to throw across some tins of cocoa and biscuits. We told him to keep for himself enough food to last for at least two months, and to occupy our tent at the base of the cliff. He would remain there as our only link with the world below.

Then we made a list of our stores. We had enough food for several weeks and plenty of tobacco, a large telescope and a pair of binoculars. We also had the four rifles, the

shotgun and 150 medium pellet cartridges. We collected all these things in a clearing and chopped down a number of thorny bushes, which we arranged in a large circle around them. This was to be our headquarters, a place of refuge in dangerous times and a guard house for our stores. We called it Fort Challenger, and our new country Maple White Land.

Then disguising the entrance with even more thorny bushes, we left our new camp for our first look at this new and dangerous world.

We had hardly started before we came across signs of the amazing things that were in store.

We began by following a little stream which flowed by our camp, thinking it would act as a guide. After following it for a few hundred yards through thick forest we entered a flat region where our stream widened into a considerable bog.

Suddenly Lord John, who had been taking the lead, halted us with an uplifted hand.

'Look at this!' he cried. 'By George, this must be the trail of the biggest bird in the world!'

An enormous three-toed track was imprinted in the soft mud before us. The creature, whatever it was, had crossed the swamp and passed on into the forest.

'I've seen these marks before,' cried Challenger. 'This is no bird, Roxton, no bird at all!'

'A beast?'

'No, a reptile – a dinosaur. Nothing else could have left such a track! But who in the world could have hoped to have seen a sight like this?' His words died away to a whisper and we all stood rooted to the spot. Following the tracks, we had left the bog and passed through a screen of brushwood and trees. Beyond was an open glade, and in it were five of the most extraordinary creatures I have ever seen. We crouched down among the bushes to watch.

Of the five of them, two were adults and three were young ones. They were quite enormous, and even the babies were as big as elephants. They had a slate-coloured skin with scales like a lizard's, and it shimmered in the sun. All five were sitting up, balancing themselves upon

their broad, powerful tails and their huge three-toed hind feet, while they used five-fingered front feet to pull down the branches of the trees that they were eating. The best way I can think of describing them is to say that they looked like monstrous kangaroos, twenty feet high, and with skins like black crocodiles.

We watched for some time as the large ones uprooted whole trees as if they were saplings. The small ones gambolled clumsily around their parents, sometimes falling over their own feet with dull and earthshaking thuds! At last one of the adults pulled up a tree that fell on its head and the great beast slowly lurched off, its small brain presumably deciding that the neighbourhood was now dangerous! It was followed by its mate and three vast infants.

I looked at my comrades. Lord John was standing, quite stupefied, his finger still on the trigger of his elephant gun. The two professors had seized each other by the hand in their excitement, and stood like two children who had been presented with a whole sweetshop.

'Merciful Heavens!' cried Summerlee, at last. 'Iguanadons! Whatever will they say in England about this?'

8 Attack of the winged reptiles

After our first meeting with the iguanadons, we became much more aware of the feeling of mystery and danger around us. In the gloom of the trees there seemed to be constant menace, and as I looked up into their shadowy foliage vague terrors crept into my heart. Although these particular monsters were obviously stupid and probably harmless, what other fiercer horrors would we find lurking in the undergrowth? I couldn't remember much about prehistoric life, but I did remember reading about flesh-eating reptiles that were a hundred times larger and fiercer than our lions. What if these were also found in the woods of Maple White Land.

Could this be really happening to me?

We now travelled more slowly and cautiously through the woods with Lord John acting as a scout, checking carefully ahead of us before letting the party advance. We had travelled two or three miles further, keeping to the right of the stream, when we came upon a large opening in the trees where a belt of brushwood led up to a tangle of rocks. As we walked slowly towards these rocks, among bushes which reached to our waists, we became aware of a strange, low gabbling and whistling sound. Lord John halted us and crept along by himself to the jagged line of rocks. He peered over the edge.

What he saw there made him look utterly astonished.
At last he recovered himself and signalled for us to follow
him. From the way he was acting it was obvious that
something wonderful but dangerous lay before us. We
crept to his side, and we looked over the rocks. It was a
pit that we found ourselves gazing into. Many years
before it might have been a volcanic crater. It was
bowl-shaped, with pools of stagnant green water at the
bottom. The place was spooky enough on its own, but its
occupants made it seem like hell itself.

It was a rookery of pterodactyls!

The bottom of the bowl was alive with young ones and
their hideous mothers, sitting on leathery yellow eggs.

From this crawling, flapping mass came the clamour we
had heard, together with a horrible, musty smell that
made us feel sick. But above, perched each upon its own
stone, tall, grey and withered, looking more dead than
alive, sat the males. They were utterly still, apart from the
rolling of their red eyes or an occasional snap of their
rat-trap beaks as a dragonfly passed them. Their huge
wings were closed by folding their fore-limbs, so that they
sat like gigantic old women, wrapped in web-coloured
shawls with ferocious heads poking out. Large and small,
not less than a thousand of these disgusting creatures lay
in the hollow before us!

Our professors would have gladly spent the day there, so

entranced were they by these weird creatures from a prehistoric age. Challenger, craning to get a better view, nearly had us all killed. He thrust his head over the rock to get a better view and caught the eye of the nearest male. It gave a shrill whistling cry, flapped its huge span of leathery wings and soared into the air. The females and young ones huddled together in the middle while the whole circle of male sentries rose one after the other and sailed off into the sky. It was a wonderful sight, but not one that we had time to enjoy.

The great monsters began to fly around us like a circle of angry bees, getting lower and lower. The dry rustling of their slate-coloured wings filled the air, and those nearest to us began to brush against our faces.

'Make for the woods and keep together,' shouted Lord John. 'These brutes mean business!'

We began to beat them off with our rifle butts, but there seemed to be nothing solid to aim at. Then suddenly a long neck shot out of the whizzing grey circle and a fierce beak snapped at us. It was followed by several more. Summerlee gave a cry and put his hand to his face, and I saw that blood was streaming from it. I felt a prod at the back of my neck and felt dizzy with shock. Challenger fell, and as I bent over him I was struck again and again from behind until I dropped on top of him.

Then I heard the crash of Lord John's elephant gun and, looking up, I saw one of the creatures struggling along the ground with a broken wing.

'Now,' cried Lord Roxton, 'run for your lives!'

We staggered through the brushwood, but before we reached the trees the harpies were on us again. Summerlee was knocked to the ground, but we dragged him up and rushed among the tree trunks. We were safe there; there was no space for those massive wings between the branches. Sore and uncomfortable we limped back to the camp. We all had nasty bites or grazes but luckily none of our injuries was serious.

'That was touch and go,' said Lord John. 'I have a horrible feeling those monsters have some sort of poison in their jaws. I didn't want to fire my gun, but there really wasn't much choice!'

'We shouldn't be here now if you hadn't,' I said. 'I think I've had enough adventures for one day!'

The day was not yet over, however, and when we reached the thorny barricade of our camp we found we had something else to worry about. The gate of Fort Challenger was untouched, the walls were unbroken. Yet in our absence it had been visited by some strange and powerful creature. Our stores had been strewn all over the ground, and one tin of meat had been crushed into pieces. A case of cartridges had been shattered to matchwood and one of the shells lay shredded beside it. Again the feeling of nameless horror crept among us and we gazed around at the dark shadows, wondering what fearsome things might be hiding in them. We felt more cheerful when we were hailed by Zambo who was sitting grinning at us from the top of the opposite pinnacle.

'All is well, Master Challenger, all is well!' he cried. 'I will stay here. You will always find me when you need me.'

His loyal, cheerful face and the immense view before us stretching half-way to the Amazon, helped to remind us that we were still living in the twentieth century, and that our nightmare was real. It was difficult to realize that

65

the violet line on the far horizon belonged to a great river on which steamers ran and people talked about everyday things. Yet my friends and I, marooned among terrifying creatures from a bygone era, could only stand and gaze and desperately long to be back there.

9 Terror in the night

Lord John Roxton was right when he thought there might
be something poisonous in the pterodactyl bites. On the
morning after the attack, both Summerlee and I had
raging temperatures and were in very great pain, while
Challenger's knee was so swollen that he could barely
limp. We stayed in the camp all that day while Lord
John did his best to strengthen the thorny walls that
protected us. I remember being constantly haunted by the
feeling that we were being closely watched. It was
uncanny. Professor Challenger put it down to the fact that
I was hot and feverish, but I became more convinced as
the day wore on that there was something evil waiting at
our very elbow. I thought again about the Indian
superstition of the *Curupuri* – the dreadful lurking spirit
of the trees. I actually began to believe in it.

That night (our third in Maple White Land) we were
grateful that Lord John had put so much work into our
defences. We were all sleeping around the dying
fire when we were woken suddenly by the most horrific
screams and cries I have ever heard in my life. They
were agonized, painful cries as earsplitting as the whistle
of a train, yet many times louder. I clapped my hands
over my ears and a cold sweat broke out all over my body.
Then another noise began, a sort of low deep-chested

laugh, – a growling throaty gurgle of merriment that made an evil accompaniment to the high-pitched shrieks. It carried on for three or four minutes and then shut off as suddenly as it began.

Lord John threw a bundle of sticks on the fire and their red glare lit up the anxious faces of my friends.

'What was it?' I whispered.

'We shall know in the morning,' said Lord John. 'It sounded very close.' Summerlee raised his hand.

'Hush,' he hissed. 'I think I heard something.'

In the deep silence we could hear a regular pit-pat. It was an animal's tread – the rhythm of soft but heavy pads placed cautiously on the ground. It stole slowly round the camp and then halted at the gateway. Now we could actually hear it breathing. Only a feeble hedge separated us from this horror of the night. What were we to do?

Lord John pulled out a small bush to make a hole in the hedge.

'Good grief,' he whispered. 'I think I can see it!'

I stooped and peered over his shoulder through the gap. Yes, I could see it too. In the deep shadow of the tree was a deeper shadow, still vague but full of savage, crouching menace. Its panting sounded as loud as a car's exhaust – it must have been colossal! Once, as it moved, I saw the glint of two terrible green eyes. There was also a frightening rustle as if it was crawling slowly forward.

'I think it's going to jump,' I said, cocking my rifle nervously.

'Don't fire! Don't fire!' whispered Lord John. 'It's too quiet. The sound of a gun will be heard for miles and we can't risk that.'

'Well, if it gets over that fence we've had it,' said Summerlee, his voice shaking with fear.

'You are absolutely right,' whispered Lord John. 'But hold your fire. I have an idea.'

He then did the bravest thing I have ever seen in my life. He picked up a blazing branch from the fire and jumped with it through a hole in the hedge. The thing ran towards him with a dreadful snarl. Without hesitating, Lord John hurled the flaming wood into the creature's face. For one second I saw a horrible mask like a giant toad's, a scabby, warty skin and a gaping mouth, dripping fresh blood. The next second there was a crash in the undergrowth and it was gone. Lord John came back laughing.

'I thought a bit of fire might scare him off,' he said.

'You should never have taken such a terrible risk!' we all shouted at him, hysterical with relief.

'Well, it was do or die,' said our hero. 'If he had got in here he would have crunched us up like nuts. It would have taken at least a dozen shots to bring down a beast that size, and in the dark we would probably have shot each other as well. What on earth was it, anyway?'

'Apart from guessing it to be a flesh-eating dinosaur, I really can't say for sure,' said Challenger. 'We may find some clues in the morning, but I think we should try and get a bit of sleep now.' After that nasty incident, we took turns at sentry duty throughout the night. We would never have dared to sleep again without a watchman.

In the morning we soon found the source of the previous night's uproar. The iguanadon glade looked like a butcher's shop. At first we thought that several animals had been killed, but when we looked more closely, it seemed as if a single iguanadon had been torn apart and the pieces scattered in every direction. The two professors examined the pieces carefully and showed us the marks

of savage teeth and enormous claws. They decided it must be either an allosaurus or a megalosaurus, two of the largest kinds of meat-eating dinosaurs. My most horrific nightmares had now been realized. Things couldn't possibly get worse!

There was one curious thing about the iguanadon remains. On the dull, scaly skin, somewhere above the shoulder, there was a single black spot of something hard and tacky that looked like asphalt. Lord John and I were mystified by this, but Professor Challenger thought it might be something to do with the highly volcanic nature of the plateau. He guessed that somewhere near at hand there was a place where asphalt existed in its liquid state. Somehow, this unfortunate iguanadon had come into contact with it.

The rest of the morning we spent mapping out part of the plateau. We avoided the pterodactyl swamp and kept to the east of our brook instead of the west. In that direction the country was still thickly wooded. The trees offered us more protection, particularly from the airborne monsters, but they made our progress very slow.

Up to now I have written a great deal about the terrors we found in Maple White Land; but there is a much happier side to it, as we found out that morning. We wandered among lovely flowers, mostly white and yellow; these being, as our professors explained, the colours of primitive flowers. In many places the ground was completely covered in them, and as we walked on a carpet ankle deep, their beautiful scent rose up to meet us. We were also pleased to see a great many homely British bees. There were trees laden with fruit, some familiar, some strange. We sampled the sort we saw the birds eating, but avoided the rest in case they were poisonous.

We saw many small animals such as porcupines, a scaly ant-eater and a wild pig with long, curving tusks. We also discovered another family of iguanadons peacefully grazing on grass and branches. Lord John, who had watched them closely through his binoculars, said they too were spotted with asphalt.

At last we returned to camp, delighted to find it undisturbed, and sat down to have a serious talk about our future plans.

Summerlee, who in the last 24 hours had returned to his bitter and acid-tempered self, opened the discussion.

'What we should really be doing, instead of wandering aimlessly about this plateau, is finding some way out of the trap we are in. You all seem to be using your brains to push us further *into* this dangerous country. I, for one, have had enough. I think it's time we got out of it. We came here on a definite mission, to test the truth of Professor Challenger's statements. The mission is complete and our work is done. We would need much more equipment and more men to launch a proper expedition. To carry on alone like this is madness. Professor Challenger got us up here. I suggest he uses his great brain to get us down again!'

I must admit I thought Summerlee's views were very reasonable. Even Challenger had to agree with him, though I think he would have been content to spend the rest of his life browsing around this dangerous place. He seemed quite fearless.

After we had discussed the subject heatedly and at some length, Challenger promised to find a way of getting off the plateau. But he would not do it, he said, until we had some sort of chart to help with the next expedition

he was going to bring! Professor Summerlee gave a snort of impatience.

'We have been exploring for two long days and we are no wiser than when we started. The whole plateau is thickly wooded and it would take months to work out the geography of it all. As you can see, the land slopes down from here; there is no central peak, it is impossible to get a proper view of it.'

It was at that moment that I had my inspiration!

10 The ape-man

I had been staring at an enormous gnarled ginko tree that cast its branches over our camp. Its trunk was exceptionally broad, and it seemed to stretch up and up to the very roof of the sky. Surely the top of this mighty tree would give an excellent view over the whole of Maple White Land?

Now, ever since I ran wild as a boy in Ireland, I have been an expert tree-climber. I may be pretty clumsy when it comes to scaling rocks, but I feel completely at home with trees. I was sure I could climb to the top of this one, high though it was. My friends were all in favour of the idea, and Lord John gave me a resounding slap on the back.

'There's only an hour or so of daylight left,' he said, 'but if you take your notebook you might be able to get a rough sketch of the place. If we put these three ammunition cases under the bottom branch, I will soon hoist you onto it!'

Lord John stood on the boxes while I faced the trunk and was gently lifting me when Challenger leapt eagerly forward and gave me such an almighty shove with his huge hand that I shot up into the tree like a rocket. Luckily the branches were well-placed for climbing and I was able to grab one and then scramble up almost as

easily as climbing a ladder. But the tree was truly gigantic.
Looking up, I could still see no sign of the branches
getting any thinner. Then I noticed a rather odd
bush-like clump on the branch over which I was crawling.
I leaned around it to have a closer look and in my surprise
and horror very nearly fell out of the tree.

A face was gazing into mine – at a distance of only a foot
or two. It was a human face, or at least far more human
than any monkey's I have ever seen. It was long, white
and blotchy with a flat nose, prominent lower jaw and a
whiskery chin. When it opened its mouth I saw it had
sharp, curved eye-teeth. Its eyes were ferocious and
filled with hate; but suddenly, for no reason I can think
of, the hate turned to fear and it disappeared amid a
swirl of leaves and branches.

'Are you all right?' came Lord John's voice faintly from below.

'Did you see it?' I shouted, hanging on to a branch for dear life, every nerve in my body tingling.

'We heard a bit of a commotion as if your foot had slipped. What was it?'

I couldn't answer. I was so shocked by the sudden appearance of the ape-man that I had to sit for a while to get my breath back. I wanted to rush back down the tree to tell them all about it, but that, I thought, would be a cowardly thing to do, especially since I had climbed so far. After a long pause, I continued to climb. Gradually I noticed the leaves thinning around me and a strong wind blowing my hair. I was now higher than any of the other trees in the forest, but I was determined not to stop until I reached the topmost branch. There I found a convenient fork and, balancing myself, looked out at the wonderful panorama of the plateau.

From this height it seemed to be an oval about 30 miles long by 20 miles wide. Its general shape was like a shallow funnel, with all the sides sloping to a large lake in the centre. This lake looked about 10 miles around, very green and beautiful, with a thick fringe of reeds at its edges and several golden sandbanks. There were long, dark objects on the sand which were too large for alligators and too long for canoes. I could see through the binoculars that they were alive, but I hadn't the faintest idea what they were. I could see the iguanadon glade just below me and further off was a round opening in the trees that marked the pterodactyl swamp.

On the other side, the plateau looked completely different. There, the red rock cliffs we had seen on the outside continued on inside the plateau, making a great ridge about 200 feet high. Just above the ground, I could see several holes in the cliffs that looked like the mouths of caves. I worked on the drawing of my chart until sundown and then carefully climbed down again.

For once I was a hero. The brilliant idea had been mine and I alone had carried it out successfully. The chart I had drawn would save us at least a month of groping round in the dark. The others were full of praise for my efforts and one after another they shook me by the hand. Then I told them about the ape-man.

'He had been there all the time,' I said.

'How do you know that?' asked Lord John.

'Because I have always had the feeling that something evil was watching us. I am convinced it was him!'

Professor Challenger was excited by my description of the ape-man and thought we must have come across the famous 'missing link' – a creature somewhere between an ape and a man. He felt it was our duty to investigate this strange creature further. But luckily Summerlee stopped him in his tracks.

'We will do nothing of the sort,' he snapped. 'Thanks to Mr Malone we have the chart you wanted. Now our only duty is to get ourselves out of this awful place as quickly and safely as possible.'

'Very well,' said Challenger. 'I must admit that I will feel happier when our friends in England hear the results of our expedition. I have no idea, as yet, how to get down from here but I promise to concentrate hard on it tomorrow. Don't worry, my friends, I shall find a way.'

11 Alone in the dark

I found it impossible to sleep that night. I was still excited
by my adventure in the tree and glowing with pride at the
way my three friends had thanked me for my bravery.
At 23 I was by far the youngest member of the party, and
had always felt ignorant and inexperienced compared with
the others. Now I had proved myself to be as much a man
as they were. It was that vain glow of self-satisfaction that
was to be my undoing. It put me in the most terrible
danger and gave me enough shocks to last me a lifetime.
If I live to be a hundred I shall never have a night as
dreadful as the one I am going to tell you about now. It
happened like this:

Summerlee was on guard, sitting hunched over a small
fire, his rifle on his knees and his pointed goat-like beard
wagging with each weary nod of his head. Lord John was
sound asleep, wrapped in his warm poncho, while
Challenger snored with a roar and a rattle that should
have kept any wild animal at bay. The moon was shining
brightly and the air was cold and crisp.

What a perfect night for a walk! And why not? What a
wonderful article it would make for *The Daily Gazette*
when we got back. 'Alone in the dark in the land of the
dinosaurs' by Edward Dunn Malone. What a scoop!
I would become a legend in the newspaper world.

It was a thought too tempting to resist, and without stopping to think again I picked up my gun and slipped through the hedge.

Summerlee, a useless sentry, was still nodding over the fire like a rusty clockwork toy. I hadn't gone a hundred yards before I regretted my stupidity. But it was my vanity that spurred me on, just as it had in the tree. I couldn't slink back into the camp after two minutes; if anyone saw me I would look a complete fool!

It was dreadful in the forest. The trees grew so thickly that I couldn't see the moonlight at all; it was as black as pitch. I thought of the tortured scream of the dying iguanadon and remembered the glimpse I had of the evil, bloodstained monster that attacked it. I was on its hunting ground; it might spring out from the shadows at any second now.

I stopped and took a cartridge from my pocket to put in my gun. As I touched the lever I nearly shouted aloud. I had brought the shotgun by mistake. As I had nothing to load it with, it was completely useless! I really must return now! I had, after all, an excellent excuse. No one could think any less of me for it. Yet again my foolish pride nagged at me. After a little hesitation I screwed up my courage and carried on, tucking the useless gun under my arm.

I had been frightened in the dark wood, but the white still flood of moonlight in the iguanadon glade was terrifying. None of the great brutes was in sight; they must be as frightened as I was. In the misty, silvery night, I could see no sign of a living thing.

I slipped across the glade quickly and found the brook that had been our guide on previous days. Its gurgling and chuckling cheered me up. I knew that as long as I followed it down, I must come to the camp. Often I lost sight of it altogether because of the tangled brushwood, but I was always within earshot of its tinkle and splash. I passed close to the pterodactyl swamp, and as I did so I heard a dry leathery rattle of wings and saw one of the great creatures silhouetted against the moon like a flying skeleton. I lay low at this point; I didn't want it to call out to its relatives!

When it settled, I crept on again. I now began to hear a low murmuring noise in front of me. It gradually grew louder, like the bubbling of a pot, until I discovered what caused it.

In the centre of a small clearing there was a pool, about as big as a Trafalgar Square fountain, of some black tarry liquid. It rose and fell in great blisters of bursting gas, and the ground around it was too hot to touch. This was where the iguanadons had found the asphalt – probably the last rumblings of a volcanic outburst that had raised the plateau in the first place.

I had no time to stop and examine it. I crept on. In the great moonlit clearings, I slunk along in the shadows. In the jungle I almost crawled. Every time a branch creaked or a twig snapped, my heart stopped beating. It was an exciting outing, but I can't honestly say that I was enjoying myself.

At last I arrived at my destination – the lake I had seen from the tree. I drank from its cool water and then climbed onto a huge block of lava nearby. Lying on top of it I had an excellent view all around. The first thing I saw amazed me! The cliffs with the caves I had seen from my tree were now lit up. I guessed they must be about ten miles away, and there were discs of light in each one like the portholes of a liner in the dark. These glowing spots of light could only mean one thing – fire. And fires could only be lit by human hands. Could there really be human beings on the plateau after all? What a story to return to London with!

I lay there for a long time watching the lights flickering in the caves and the animals coming to drink at the lake. There were creatures like giant armadillos, and a huge stag with branching horns that brought its doe and two fawns to the lakeside.

Suddenly they all scuttled for shelter. A newcomer, an animal under whose tremendous weight the ground shook, was coming down the path. As it advanced I wondered why its vast shape looked so familiar, its arched back with triangular fringes and a strange bird-like head held close to the ground. Then I remembered the drawing in Maple White's sketchbook. Of course, this was the stegosaurus!

For five minutes the creature stood and drank, so close to my rock that I could have leaned over and touched it. Then it lumbered away and was lost among the boulders.

Looking at my watch, I saw it was half-past two. Time I started back! I felt very pleased with myself – how amazed my friends would be when I told them all my news!

Returning was far easier than setting out had been, and I was eagerly plodding up a slope about half-way home when I heard a strange noise some distance behind me. It was somewhere between a growl and a snarl – low, deep and very threatening. An icy finger tickled my spine and I began to run. I had gone about half a mile when the noise was repeated, still behind me but a great deal louder. My heart stood still as I realized that this was not a beast that happened to be passing but something that was actually *tracking me*! I felt my scalp tingle and my hair.

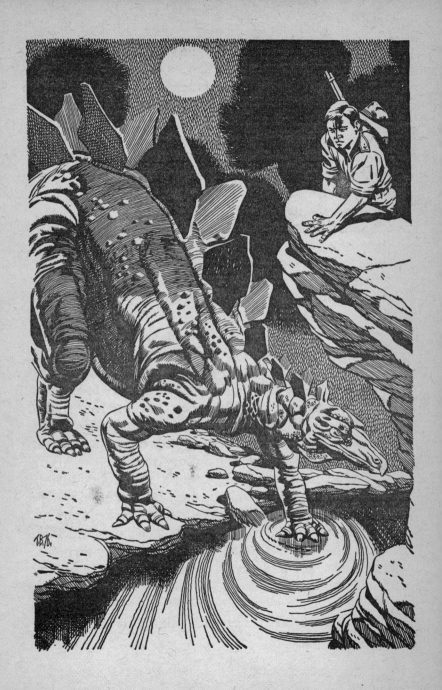

stand on end, and once more the vision of the iguanadon-killer, lit up by torch-light, flashed before my eyes.

With my knees knocking, I turned and stared down the moonlit path behind me. All was quiet and still. I could see nothing. Then, out of the silence came that low, throaty croaking, but far louder and closer than before. I nearly fainted. Something dreadful was on my tail and was fast closing in on me! Rooted to the spot, I continued to stare along the path behind me.

Then I saw it.

There was a movement in the bushes at the far end of the path. A great dark shadow hopped out into the bright moonlight. For a second I hoped that it was a peaceful iguanadon, but as I stared I could see that this was a completely different creature. Instead of the gentle, deer-shaped head of the leaf-eaters we had seen in the glade, this beast had a broad, squat, toad-like face. His ferocious cry and the speed at which he was chasing me left me in no doubt as to what he would like for his supper. It was a flesh-eating dinosaur, my nightmare come to life, and one of the most terrifying beasts ever to have walked the earth. As the huge creature loped along it dropped onto its forepaws and every few yards or so put its nose to the ground. It was smelling out my trail!

What on earth could I do? I looked round for a tree to climb, but there were only bushes. My last hope was to run. I left the rough, broken ground by the brook and began to sprint along a flat, hard-beaten animal track where I had less chance of tripping and falling on my face. I flung my useless gun away and ran until I felt my throat would burst and my legs would no longer hold me. I thought I had thrown him off. The path behind me was silent. And then suddenly, with a thudding of giant feet

and a panting of monster lungs, the beast was on me once
more. I was lost.

As he came round a curve in the path the moonlight
shone on his huge, bulbous eyes, the rows of enormous
teeth and the gleaming fringe of claws on his short
forepaws. With a scream of terror, I rushed headlong
down the path, expecting at every second to feel his talons
tearing at my shoulders. Then I heard a crash and found
myself flying through space.

After that there was only darkness and rest.

12 Ransacked camp

I wasn't unconscious for long, probably only a few minutes, but as I came round I was aware of the most dreadful and penetrating smell. I felt around in the darkness and my hands closed over a large bone and a huge lump of meat. Above me there was a circle of starlit sky, which showed me that I was lying at the bottom of a deep pit. I got to my feet with difficulty and was delighted to find that, although I was bruised and battered, my bones seemed to be unbroken. Nor was there any sign of the monster – I could hardly believe my luck!

I had a box of matches in my pocket and I struck one to see where I had ended up. It didn't need much light to show me quite clearly that I was in a large, man-made animal trap. It was a pit with sharply sloping walls and a level bottom about 20 feet across. The bottom was littered with putrid lumps of animal flesh, which accounted for the horrible smell. In the centre was a greased pole, about nine feet long and sharpened to a point. It was stained dark red with the blood of the animals that had been impaled upon it. I remembered that Challenger had said man could not exist on this plateau. Well, he seemed to me to be making a very good job of it; hiding in caves by night and setting clever traps on animal paths by day.

Even amid the dreadful dangers of this plateau, man had obviously found a way to survive.

The sloping walls of the pit were not too difficult for me to climb, but I was still worried that the dinosaur might be lurking outside. I scrambled to the edge and looked over. Dawn was breaking and I could feel the cold wind of morning blowing on my face. I slowly clambered out and, taking courage in both hands, stole back along the path, picking up my gun on the way. At last I found the brook again and, with many frightened backward glances, made for home.

As I hurried on my way, I was surprised to hear a rifle-shot coming from the direction of the camp. Thinking my absence had been discovered, I rushed along even faster to tell my friends that I was safe. But I was weary and stiff and my legs would not move as quickly as I should have liked.

At last I was at the open gate of Fort Challenger. A fearful sight met my eyes. Our belongings, including rifles, were scattered over the ground in wild confusion, and my comrades had disappeared. Close to the ashes of the fire the grass was stained crimson by a large pool of blood.

I was so stunned by this sudden shock that for a while I went completely berserk. I rushed round the empty camp, screaming and wailing for my companions. For all my bravery and cleverness, I now realized just how much I had leaned on the others. Without them I was like a child lost in the dark, completely helpless. Suddenly I remembered Zambo. Perhaps I was not completely alone in the world. I went to the edge of the plateau and, sure enough, he was down below, squatting among his blankets beside the fire in his little camp. I waved to him and in a short time he had climbed the pinnacle to talk to me. He listened to my story with deep distress.

'Devil got them, sure, Master Malone,' he said. 'Do as I say and come out of there.'

'But how can I, Zambo?' I asked.

'I have an idea, master,' he told me. 'One of the Indians has come back to see how we are. I could send him to the village for ropes and perhaps we could make some sort of bridge out of them!'

That evening I threw Zambo my purse which contained three English sovereigns, a letter for Mr McArdle and a note asking for help. It was to be given to any English-speaking man the Indian could find. I promised to pay the Indian twice as much if he would return with the ropes. As the sun was setting, I saw his lonely figure, my one faint hope of salvation, making his way across the plain beneath us.

I wasn't looking forward to my first night alone in the looted camp, but after lighting three fires and carefully closing the gate I was so exhausted that I fell almost at once into a deep sleep. As dawn broke the next day I was overjoyed to be shaken awake by the hand of my dear friend, Lord Roxton. But it wasn't the Lord John I remembered. The man standing over me was pale and wild-eyed with a scratched, bloody face and clothes that hung in rags. I stared in amazement, but he gave me no time for questions.

'Quick, quick!' he cried. 'Get the rifles and all the cartridges you can find. Fill up your pockets. Now, grab some food. Half a dozen tins will do. Don't wait to talk or think. Get a move on, or we've had it!' Still half awake, I hurried around, madly following his instructions, and then rushed after him as he left the camp. We ran and

ran until we found a large clump of brushwood some distance away.

'There!' he panted. 'I think we are safe here. They will go straight to the camp.'

'Who will?' I gasped. 'And where are the professors?'

'The ape-men, of course,' he cried. 'My God, what brutes! Don't raise your voice; they have long ears. But where do you think you've been, young Ned?' I told him the story of my dreadful night and he, in turn, told me his.

At daybreak, hordes of the ferocious ape-men had leapt down from the big ginko tree and captured them. Lord John had managed to shoot one, which accounted for the blood I had seen. Although they had treated Summerlee and Lord John pretty badly and dragged them through clumps of brambles, they had taken a great liking to hairy Professor Challenger, who seemed to bear a strange likeness to their chief. He had been carried shoulder-high and treated very well.

Lord John broke off his story as we heard a strange noise in the distance like the clicking of castanets.

'There they go!' said my friend, loading up his rifle. 'That's the noise they make when they're excited. Anyway, Ned,' he continued, 'they took us to their village about four miles from here near the cliffs. There were about a thousand huts made of branches and leaves. They tied up Summerlee and me and left us, but old Challenger was up a tree having the time of his life. He was hob-nobbing with his twin brother, the chief ape-man, eating fruit and singing his head off. They let him do just what he liked!'

'The surprising thing though, Ned, was that there were other human captives there. They were small fellows with reddish-brown skins, and they had been bitten and

clawed so badly they could barely walk. But they were
very plucky men and just stood there bravely, never once
wailing or pleading for mercy! Apparently the humans
hold one side of the plateau, in the area of the caves, and
the ape-men the side where we pitched our camp. A war
seems to go on between them the whole time.'

He stopped again and we listened intently, but the forest
was peaceful and still. Lord John went on with his story.

'You had a lucky escape, young fellow. Do you remember
that great bristle of bamboo canes where we saw the
skeleton of the American? Well, that seems to be the
ape-men's execution ground. There are probably dozens
more skeletons in the bamboo if we had stopped to look
further. They marched us all over to have a look at it and
made four of the Indians jump off the top. The canes went

through them like knitting needles through butter. It was a sickening, horrible sight, particularly as we thought it was our turn next! But Summerlee and I were being saved up to star in today's performance. That's why I thought it was time to make a break for it. I had to do it myself. Summerlee is worse than useless and Challenger isn't much better. I kicked my guardian in the stomach this morning and here I am.'

'But what about the professors?' I cried.

'Well, we have to go back and collect them, of course. Now we have the rifles it should be child's play. The ape-men don't understand guns, thank heavens!'

13 Two narrow escapes

After breakfasting quickly from one of the tins, we set off for the ape-men's village. We crept carefully through the woods which seemed to be full of the clicking chatter of those shaggy ginger creatures, but fortunately we didn't bump into any. At last we arrived at a clearing, around which grew a semi-circle of large trees. Among the branches hundreds of tiny huts had been built, and at the moment they seemed to be inhabited by the female ape people and their babies. In the open, near the edge of the cliff, there was a crowd of about a hundred red-haired males, many of them of immense size and all of them rather ugly. In front stood a little group of Indians, small and handsome, their skin glowing like polished bronze in the strong sunlight. A thin, dejected white man stood near them – unmistakably Professor Summerlee.

The group of prisoners were closely guarded by the ape-men, but further towards the edge of the cliff I saw a strange and fascinating couple. One was our Professor Challenger. The remains of his coat still hung from his shoulders, but his shirt was gone and his great beard was tangled all over his mighty chest. He had lost his hat and his wild hair was standing on end. A single day seemed to have changed him from a civilized man to a desperate savage. Beside him stood the king of the apes, looking

the very image of the professor except that his hair was red instead of black. They had the same shaped body and tangled beard, – in fact the only difference between them was the chief's ape-like skull.

I had only a few seconds to observe this before two of the ape-men suddenly rushed forward, seized an Indian, and threw him over the precipice. They hurled him with such force that he curved high in the air before dropping with a hideous scream onto the pointed bamboo. Then they grabbed Summerlee. His poor, thin figure fluttered and struggled like a chicken being pulled from its coop. Challenger had turned to the king and was obviously pleading for his colleague's life. The ape-man threw the professor roughly to one side. It was the last thing he ever did! Lord John's rifle cracked out and the ape-king fell, a tangled red thing, onto the ground.

'Shoot as many as you can!' cried my friend. I hated pulling the trigger, but knew I had no choice if we were to survive. They came at us from all directions, but with four guns between us we had the advantage. Challenger grabbed the bewildered Summerlee and, hand in hand, they ran towards us. The three of us then made for the brushwood hiding-place while Lord John covered our retreat with his rifle. When at last we arrived at the hiding-place, we found the four surviving Indians had also escaped and had been running close behind. The poor things were trembling with fear, and we pulled them inside with us.

'We must look after them,' said Summerlee, who was puffing at his pipe and obviously feeling much better. 'You've pulled us out of the jaws of death today, boys. It was an amazing bit of work and I'm very grateful to you. I really thought my last moments had come!'

The following morning we decided that the only possible plan was to take the Indians back to their own people. We knew that the caves would be much safer for all of us, and the fact that we had saved the lives of four of their tribe should surely earn us a warm reception. The men we had rescued were wiry, active and very good-humoured. They wore leather loin cloths and had long, straight black hair, tied back with leather thongs. Although we were unable to talk to them, except by signs, they spoke fluently among themselves. Their tribe seemed to be called Accala. The youngest one, a very spirited youth, appeared to be their leader.

We had, till then, been pretty sure that the ape-men were no longer on our trail. But I began to suspect the worst when one of the Indians went to get water from the

brook and didn't return. I took my rifle and went to look for him. I found him huddled in the bushes. He was quite dead, and his head seemed to have been almost screwed off. I gave a cry to warn the others and bent over to pick up the body. As I did so, two huge paws closed over my neck and throat and I was gently lifted off the ground. The next moment I felt an unbearable pressure forcing my head back against my spine. Although my senses were reeling, I was aware of two cold blue eyes looking into mine. They were hypnotic and terrible, and, for the second time in two days, I felt darkness closing over me. Little silvery bells began to tinkle in my ears and somewhere in the distance I heard the crack of a rifle.

I awoke to find myself back on the grass in my brush-wood lair. Someone had brought water from the brook and my face was being sprinkled with it. Luckily Lord John had heard my cry and had shot the ape in the back. Another second and the brute would have snapped my neck like a twig.

It was clear now that the apes knew exactly where we were and were watching us carefully. I shivered – the sooner we left this side of the plateau the better.

14 Council of war

We left in the early morning with the young chief walking in front. While the others would help us to carry our provisions, he tossed his head proudly and refused to carry anything. I trudged along behind and could not help smiling at the appearance of my three companions. No three tramps could have looked more helpless and bedraggled. They had all lost their hats and had handkerchiefs knotted around their heads to protect them from the sun. Their clothes hung in ribbons and their grimy, unshaven faces were quite unrecognizable. Challenger and Summerlee were limping badly while I could barely move my poor neck, it was so bruised and sore. We were certainly an odd-looking little band and I wasn't surprised to see the Indians eyeing us warily from time to time!

We reached the lake by late afternoon, and there a wonderful sight met our tired eyes. A whole flotilla of canoes was sweeping across the glassy surface towards us. As soon as they recognized the Indians the men in the canoes let out a thunderous roar of delight. We saw them standing up in the boats, waving their spears and paddles in the air. The canoes almost flew across the last stretch of water and as soon as they reached the shore the Indians leapt out and threw themselves at our feet with loud cries

of greeting. An older man, wearing jewellery and animal skins, rushed forward and hugged the young chief very tenderly.

It was obvious that the natives were on the warpath, for every man carried a spear – a long bamboo tipped with bone – and either a club or a stone battle axe. It seemed that our young friend was the chief's son, and we had just bumped into a war party going to his rescue.

The young chief spoke to his tribesmen for a long time and it was obvious from the dark, angry faces that the ape-men had this time overstepped the mark. Then the whole tribe squatted in a circle for what appeared to be a council of war. We sat on a nearby slab of rock and watched with interest. We didn't need to know the language to realize that the Indians were shocked and angered by the young chief's story. Their tribesmen had

been murdered, and there was a score to be settled. The war party would not be returning home but advancing to attack the ape-people. It was made clear by the old chief that we, with our 'thunder-sticks', would be going with them.

It was too late to advance that night, so we built fires and settled where we were. Some of the Indians brought a young iguanadon out of the jungle and within minutes it had been cut into slabs and was hanging, roasting over a dozen camp fires. Challenger and Summerlee enjoyed being in camp by the lake and watching the amazing variety of life in its rose-tinted waters. An astonishing creature wriggled onto a sandbank quite near us. It had a barrel-shaped body, a serpent-like neck and flippers.

'A fresh-water plesiosaurus!' cried Summerlee. 'What a sight! We must be the luckiest of zoologists since the world began!'

Our camp broke up before dawn and we set out on an expedition I shall never forget. More tribesmen from the caves had joined us during the night, and there were now four or five hundred of us. Roxton and Summerlee had been put on the right flank, while Challenger and I were on the left.

We had not long to wait for our enemy. A wild, shrill clamour rose from the edge of the woods and a group of ape-men rushed out with clubs and stones. It was a brave move but a foolish one, for the Indians were very much faster on their feet and skilled at fighting with spears. It was over in minutes, without a shot being fired.

We pressed onward into the jungle and for an hour or more the struggle became desperate. The ape-men, in their element among trees, surprised us many times by springing out of the branches. Several warriors were

108

clubbed to the ground. But at last the apes realized that they were outnumbered, and the survivors rushed away through the brushwood in all directions, pursued by the men with savage shouts of delight.

'It's all over!' said Lord John. 'I think we can leave the rest of the tidying up to them.'

Free of the menace of the ape-people, we were now able to return to our camp and collect our stores. We were also able to speak to Zambo, who had been terrified by the noise of fighting he had heard from the plateau.

'Come away, masters, come away!' he cried, his eyes wide with fear. 'The devil get you sure if you stay up there!'

'That man is absolutely right,' said Summerlee. 'That's the most sensible thing I've heard this week. I tell you, Challenger, from now on you will devote every waking moment to getting us out of this horrible country and back to dear old London again!'

15 Tunnel to freedom

Some day, when I have a better desk than a meat tin and a more useful tool than a worn stub of pencil, I will write a full account of our life among the Accala Indians. After the defeat of the ape-men, they regarded us with a mixture of fear and gratitude. We made a new camp at the foot of the cliffs near their caves. The Accalans were now more than friendly towards us but would do nothing to help with our plans for leaving the plateau. Any suggestion from us that they might lend ropes or planks of wood to build our bridge met with a refusal. They would smile and shake their heads, and that was the end of it. The only one who seemed sorry for us was the young chief we had rescued. He told us by sign language that he would like to help us but dared not. Apparently since the defeat of the ape-men, we were considered to be lucky mascots! If we were to leave it would be a bad omen for the Accalan tribe.

In the days we spent with the Accalans we saw many amazing things. We learned that the iguanadons were were kept as tame herds by their owners and were simply used as walking meat stores. We were impressed by the men's skill at hunting, trapping and harpooning, and the ordered and happy way in which they organized their lives in the caves. On the third day, however, we discovered that man was still not the complete master of the plateau. We saw a group of at least a dozen Indians being set upon and eaten by two of the carnivorous dinosaurs of my nightmares. There was nothing we could do to help; our guns made little impact on their towering bulk. The Indians had their own way of killing them – peppering them all over with poisoned darts. Unfortunately, the poison took a long time to work and most of the group of Indians had been crushed or mangled to death before the great monsters were toppled. The problem of these massive meat-eaters was obviously always present and made life very insecure for the Indians.

In spite of this constant threat, I had twice been back alone to our old camp to have a word with Zambo. By now I hoped he would have news of the Indian. But the plain beneath the pinnacle stretched away, empty and desolate to the distant horizon.

It was on the way back from one of these trips that I saw a very strange object approaching me. It was a man walking along inside a bell-shaped framework of bent bamboo canes – rather like a cage. As I drew nearer I was astonished to see that it was Lord John Roxton! When he saw me he got out from under it and smiled rather sheepishly.

'Well, young fellow,' he said. 'Fancy seeing you here!'

'What on earth do you think you are doing?' I asked.

'Oh, just visiting my friends the pterodactyls,' he said. 'I rigged this up to stop them biting me.'

'But why?' He avoided my eyes and muttered something about getting a pterodactyl chick for Challenger to study. With this he squeezed back into the cage and went off to the swamp, promising to be back by nightfall.

112

A couple of weeks later our fortunes took a turn for the
better. One evening, after dusk, the young chief came
down to our little camp, handed me a small roll of tree
bark and pointed to a row of caves above his head. He
then put his finger to his lips as a sign of secrecy and stole
away as quietly as he had come. We were mystified by his
behaviour and we examined the tree bark very carefully
in the glow from the fire. It was about a foot square and
inside there was an arrangement of lines drawn in charcoal
on the moist white surface. Lord John was the first to
have an inkling of its meaning.

'By George!' he cried. 'I think I've got it! Look – there
are 18 marks on the paper and 18 openings in the cliffs
above us. It's obviously some sort of chart of the caves.
The mark with the cross must mean it is different from
the rest.'

'One that goes out through the cliff!' I shouted in my
excitement.

'I think our young friend has solved the riddle,' said
Challenger. 'And as the caves above our heads are used as
store-houses there are no Accalans around. I vote we go
and spy out the land!'

Each one of us picked up a faggot of wood and made our
way up the weed-covered steps to the cave that was marked
in the drawing. It was, as we had hoped, quite empty,
except for many enormous bats that flapped around our
heads as we stumbled along in the dark. We dared not
light our torches until we had gone some distance into the
tunnel.

It was a beautiful, dry tunnel, with smooth grey walls
and a curved roof. We hurried along it eagerly until, with
a deep groan of disappointment, we were brought to a

halt. A sheer wall of rock had appeared before us, without a chink even big enough for a mouse. There was no escape for us there. I looked at the map again and realized what had happened. The passage was slightly forked and in the darkness we had taken the wrong turning. We retraced our steps and sure enough, thirty yards further back a great black opening loomed in the wall. We turned and ran, breathless with excitement, headlong down it! Then we saw a pin-prick of flame, growing larger and larger as we hurried towards it. It looked like a great curtain glowing before us, silvering the cave and turning the sand to powdered jewels.

'The moon, by George!' cried Lord John. 'We are through, boys, we are through!'

It was indeed the full moon that shone straight into our window-sized opening in the cliffs. As we looked over the edge we could see that the climb down was not going to be difficult as we were a lot nearer the ground than we had hoped.

The following night, with a few belongings, our rifles and a large box of Challenger's (the contents of which were a secret), we entered the tunnel for the last time. From the slope below us rose the voices of the Indians as they laughed and sang. As we hesitated, the call of some weird animals rang clearly out of the darkness. It was the very voice of Maple White Land, our land, bidding us goodbye. We turned and plunged into the cave which led to home.

Two hours later we, and all our packages, were at the foot of the cliffs and walking round to Zambo's camp. We were astonished and delighted to find not one fire but a dozen on the plain. The flames glowed in welcoming dots like candles on a birthday cake. The rescue party had arrived. There were twenty river Indians with many stakes and ropes. Well, at least we would have no difficulty in carrying our packages on the morrow when we started our trek back to the Amazon.

We were bursting with excitement, especially me. For the first time for ages I could actually imagine the moment when I would shake Mr McArdle by the hand!

16 A surprise package

For all the excitement we caused as we travelled through South America, we had no idea of the uproar that was to greet us when we arrived in Europe. We found Southampton packed with pressmen, but we steadfastly refused to make any comment, having decided to say nothing until we had presented our report to the Zoological Institute. The meeting had been fixed for the evening of November 7th, two days after our arrival back.

The tickets for this event were supposed to be sold only to members and friends, but long before 8 o'clock every seat in the hall was occupied. Non-members, angry at being left outside, stormed the doors at a quarter to eight after a long street fight in which several people, including a police inspector, were injured. By the time we arrived it was estimated that five thousand people had somehow crowded into the building. From the minute we stepped onto the platform we were treated like heroes. Nearly everyone in the hall stood and cheered for several minutes. I must say we all looked a great deal more attractive than we had on the plateau. We were all four neatly dressed, deeply tanned and a lot more relaxed!

After a short introduction from the chairman, Professor Summerlee rose to his feet and gave the audience a full account of our travels and our arrival on the plateau. He told how we had become marooned there and of the adventures and horrors that followed. To the interested zoologists he gave a list of 46 beetles and 174 butterflies that were completely new species. He also told of many new species of animals, completely unknown to man.

It was when he went on to describe the larger animals, the leftovers from the Jurassic period, that the bulk of the audience began to sit up and take notice. He told them of the huge iguanadons, the stegosaurus and the terrible dinosaurs, and how we had suffered from the bites of the pterodactyls. In fact he told the whole story, including our adventures with the Indians and the ape-people, in such a clear and reasonable way that I had to keep pinching myself to make sure that it was true. It just didn't seem possible that all this was happening to someone as ordinary as me!

Professor Summerlee finished his story to the sound of cheering and stamping. The audience was wild with delight. That was when the trouble started.

A Dr Illingworth of Edinburgh rose to his feet.

'I have no desire to be offensive,' he shouted above the din, 'but where is the evidence for all these wonderful tales? You cannot really expect intelligent people to believe all this with only a few photographs for proof? Photographs can easily be faked, and you seem to have nothing better to show us. A dinosaur skull or even an odd bone might have been slightly more convincing.'

A large section of the audience expressed their disgust by noisy shouts of 'Shut up!' and 'Throw him out!' A smaller section however, seemed to be of the same opinion as the doctor. It was fortunate that there were many ladies in the audience, otherwise we would have had a riot on our hands.

But suddenly there was a pause in the shouting, a hush

and then complete silence. Professor Challenger, with his swelling chest and aggressive beard, had bounced to his feet.

'Many of you present will remember the rude behaviour of certain people at the last meeting I attended here,' his voice rang out. 'One of these men was Professor Summerlee who stands before you now as thoroughly convinced as I am, having seen the plateau with his own eyes. As he has already explained, our camp was wrecked by the ape-men and most of our films were ruined.' (Jeers, laughter and 'Tell us another one!' from the back). 'However we have some good ones left, Dr Illingworth. I can show you a picture of a pterodactyl from my portfolio that would convince you beyond a doubt that —'

'No picture of a pterodactyl could convince us of anything,' said Dr Illingworth. Professor Challenger was suspiciously calm.

'Do you mean to say,' he said, 'that you would have to see the thing itself before you would believe us?'

'Undoubtedly!'

'And you would accept that as proof?' said the professor quietly. Dr Illingworth gave a shout of laughter. 'Beyond any doubt at all,' he said.

At a signal from Challenger, I rose to my feet and went to the back of the platform where Zambo was waiting for me. Together we carried forward a heavy packing case and placed it by the professor's chair.

You could have heard a pin drop in that huge hall, and every eye in the place was firmly riveted on the mysterious wooden box. Our professor slid off the lid and peered down into it, snapping his fingers and calling in a coaxing voice.

'Come on pretty, pretty,' he wheedled, 'come on, my pretty thing.' An instant later, with a loud scratching and rattling sound, a strange and loathsome thing appeared from below and perched on the side of the box.

Even the sight of the Duke of Durham falling head first into the orchestra pit could not distract the attention of the horrified audience. The face of the creature was like an ugly gargoyle created by a mad, medieval builder. It was malicious and evil, with two small red eyes as bright as burning coals. Its long, savage mouth, held half-open, was filled with a double row of shark-like teeth. Its shoulders were humped, and round them was draped what appeared to be a faded grey shawl. For the audience it was their childhood dream of a devil come to life!

There was pandemonium in the hall. Men screamed, women fainted and the other people on the platform with us tried to join the Duke in the orchestra pit. For a moment I thought there would be complete panic, but Challenger threw up his arms to quieten the throng.

That seemed to have an effect on the audience, but the sudden movement alarmed the creature beside him. Its strange shawl suddenly unfurled. It spread and fluttered into a pair of leathery wings. Challenger grabbed at its legs, but too late! The creature had sprung from its perch and was slowly circling the Queen's Hall with a dry, leathery flapping of its ten-foot wings, while the hideous smell of putrid fish filled the air. The terrified cries of the people in the galleries lashed the poor creature into a frenzy. It flew faster and faster, beating its wings against the chandeliers like a moth round a candle flame.

'The window! For heaven's sake shut that window!' shouted the professor, dancing up and down and wringing his hands. Too late! The panic-stricken monster had

found the opening, squeezed through and was gone.

Professor Challenger fell back in his chair and buried his face in his hands, while the audience breathed the loudest sigh of relief I have ever heard.

I have difficulty in remembering what happened after that, but I do remember my friends and I being carried above the heads of the crowd, through the hall and out into the street. Gathered outside I was amazed to see at least a hundred thousand people, all waiting for a glimpse of us!

'A procession! A procession!' shouted the voices. And so the crowd set off with us perched on high. As far as I can remember, we took a route through Regent Street,

Pall Mall, St James's Street and Piccadilly. The entire traffic of central London was held up, with many collisions reported between the demonstrators on one side and the police and taxi-drivers on the other. At last, after a loud chorus of 'For they are jolly good fellows', we were put down at midnight outside Lord John's apartment in the Albany.

As for the London pterodactyl, I'm afraid I can tell you nothing definite about the poor thing's fate. Two frightened ladies told how it perched on the roof of the Queen's Hall and sat as if turned to stone. Apart from that, there is only the evidence of the log of the ss Freisland, a Dutch American liner, which tells of being passed at 9 a.m. the following morning by something that was a cross between a flying goat and a monstrous bat. It was flying very fast indeed and heading south west, in the vague direction of South America.

As for me, life in London does seem rather dull after the dear old plateau, even though I am very well thought of at the office of the *Daily Gazette*. And I have a sneaking feeling that if another expedition ever does set out for the Lost World, I just might be on it!

Marie Herbert
Great Polar Adventures 40p

Eleven thrilling stories of men who risked their lives to get to the ends of
the earth. The quest for the Poles started as early as Elizabethan times but
they have only been properly explored in the last few years. Wallie
Herbert's story is included in this collection and you can plot the routes on
the maps he has drawn.

Carey Miller
Submarines! 40p

Hazardous missions, daring exploits and rescue operations are retold in
this book of true submarine stories.

Airships and Balloons 40p

Amazing tales of airships and balloons, from the one-man hot-air
balloons of the 18th century to the huge hydrogen-filled Zeppelins
of World War 1.

Baffling Mysteries 35p

Fourteen tales of mysteries that have never been solved, from the
hoofmarks of the Devonshire Devil to the last flight of Amelia
Earhart.

Alexander Barrie
Jungle Run	50p
Fly for Three Lives	45p
Operation Midnight	45p
Let Them All Starve	45p

Four exciting adventures about Jonathan Kane.

Jonathan really gets his holiday job at the Lonehead Flying Field so
that he can find out more about planes and learn to fly. But he finds
himself plunged into adventures with stelen planes, flying bullets,
a cut-throat team of political gangsters, missions to Africa and a
thrilling prison rescue.

Arthur C. Clarke
Dolphin Island 40p

This exciting story is set in the 21st century on an island in the Great
Barrier Reef. Johnny, who has run away from home and hidden aboard an
inter-continental hovership, is ship-wrecked in the middle of the South
Pacific Ocean. Stranded on a raft, he is miraculously propelled by a pack
of dolphins towards the famous centre for dolphin research. Johnny is
allowed to stay on the island and assist in training the dolphins. He goes
skin-diving at night, survives a fearful hurricane and unearths a horrifying
underwater conspiracy.

Joan Phipson
The Cats 60p

Jim couldn't help telling everyone when he won the lottery. And
that's why he and his brother were kidnapped. The car was headed
out into the wild country of the Australian bush. But the bush has a
way of turning the tables. Miles from anywhere, the kidnappers
become the victims of a wild and terrible enemy that lurks in the
mist . . .

Frank Walker
Vipers & Co 60p

Agatha Viper is the wickedest witch in all of London Town. From
her luxury office at the top of Centre Point, in league with her
husband Lancelot, MP for Wormwood and Dry Rot, she plans her
campaign to swamp the city with Gloom, Despondency and
Uglification . . . can Clare and Jonathan, caught up in a mind-
boggling series of adventures, thwart the tidal wave of nastiness
master-minded by Agatha and her associates?

Penelope Lively
A Stitch in Time 60p

Maria likes to be by herself, holding conversations in her head and
perhaps that's why she notices such strange things in the house at
Lyme Regis where she's spending the summer. There's only a cat
in the house but she can hear a dog barking. She finds a sampler
stitched a century ago by a girl called Harriet. Maria realizes that
something strange happened to Harriet, and Harriet's presence
seems uneasily close . . .

John Gilbert
Highwaymen and Outlaws 40p

Here are the terrible exploits of all the best-known outlaws and highwaymen from Captain Hind's ambush of Cromwell to the beautifully planned Great Train Robbery of 1963.

John Gilbert
Pirates and Buccaneers 40p

Read the true stories of twenty-four of the infamous pirates who have made history by their dash and lawlessness. Such ruthless and bloodthirsty captures can never cease to shock and fascinate.

Geoffrey Palmer and Noel Lloyd
Stories of Robin Hood 40p

Hidden away deep in Sherwood Forest, Robin Hood and his merry men lead a life of adventure, fun and danger. There is the story of how Robin Hood first met Little John, how Will Stutely was saved from the gallows, the wedding of Allan-a-Dale, and eight other tales.

George Laycock
Strange Monsters and Great Searches 35p

Over the centuries many strange monsters are supposed to have been seen, or thought to exist, such as the giant octopus with tentacles 100 feet long; the coelacanth, a creature that should be extinct but isn't; or the Abominable Snowman who leaves giant footprints in the snow. You can read all about these wonderful monsters in this book and about the exciting and dangerous attempts to find them.

Richard Garrett
They Must Have Been Crazy 50p

A collection of mad ideas and daring exploits, such as shooting the Niagara Falls in a barrel, or trying to fly in a flying boat with nine wings and eight engines!

Richard Garrett
Narrow Squeaks 50p

Twenty-eight enthralling real-life stories of escape from disaster and death against all the odds —

The man who jumped from a plane three and a half miles up . . . and survived!

The girl who couldn't swim, was carried out to sea . . . and stayed afloat!

The climber on the Matterhorn who survived when the rope broke and his companions fell to their deaths!

Mollie Hunter
The Thirteenth Member 60p

In the Scotland of 1590, there were many who worshipped the Prince of Darkness, and a dark night brought the Devil himself riding to meet them. Young Adam was horrified to find that Gilly, the little kitchenmaid, was the thirteenth member of a witches' coven. What was worse, the witches planned the death of Scotland's king and to stop them could mean sending Gilly to the stake . . .

Rosemary Sutcliffe
The Chief's Daughter 50p

Long, long ago, the fierce Irish sea-raiders crossed the water to ravage and plunder the coast of Wales. It was on one of these raids that Welsh tribesmen captured Dara, the boy warrior, and now the tribe's priest demands that he be killed. Dara must die as a sacrifice to the great black goddess whose anger has made the springs run dry. His only hope is Nellan, the chief's daughter who will even defy her father to save Dora's life . . .

Henry Treece
The Bronze Sword 50p

All his life Drucus had been a soldier in the ranks of Caesar's legions. But now the old centurion had hung up his weapons and settled to the quiet life of a farmer in the distant land of Britain under the rule of Rome. Suddenly, the years of the sword had returned. Boudicca and her fierce tribesmen had come to raid and pillage. The young warrior with the bronze sword brings him the Queen's verdict on whether he is to live or die . . .

Deborah Manley
Finding Out 75p

A guide to information-gathering for young readers. Whatever your hobby or interest, whatever special projects you do at school, this book – packed with advice, ideas and explanations – is a book you'll use over and over again . . . every time you need to find something out for yourself. This guide includes : reference books ; dictionaries ; atlases, maps and fieldwork ; delving into the past ; getting the best out of the library ; using numbers, graphs and statistics.

Michael Harvey and Rae Compton
Crochet Things 70p

If you think crochet sounds difficult, you're in for a surprise! This exciting craft book will show you just how easy it is. You'll soon be an expert, able to crochet things for all the family, clothes, toys and even special gifts for birthdays and Christmas.

Jennifer Laing
Buried Treasure 60p

Join the hunt for hidden hoards! From the Cullinan Diamond, the stone they called the Star of Africa, to the riches that legend tells of in the Tombs of the Scythian Blood Drinkers, *Buried Treasure* tells a host of thrilling tales of the world's hidden treasures and the adventurers who were brave or crazy enough to seek them out. And there's a special section on how to find treasure for yourself.

You can buy these and other Piccolo Books from booksellers and newsagents ; or direct from the following address :
Pan Books, Sales Office, Cavaye Place, London SW10 9PG
Send purchase price plus 20p for the first book and 10p for each additional book, to allow for postage and packing
Prices quoted are applicable in the UK

While every effort is made to keep prices low, it is sometimes necessary to increase prices at short notice. Pan Books reserve the right to show on covers and charge new retail prices which may differ from those advertised in the text or elsewhere